MAX CHASE

Illustrated by Sam Hadley

LONDON NEW DELHI NEW YORK SYDNEY

MILKY WAY

HYPERSPACE
BYPASS

INTERGALACTIC
HIGHWAY

RIGEL

IF SPACE
STATION

KORING

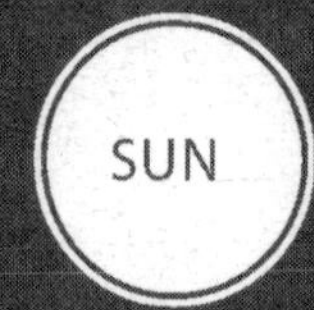

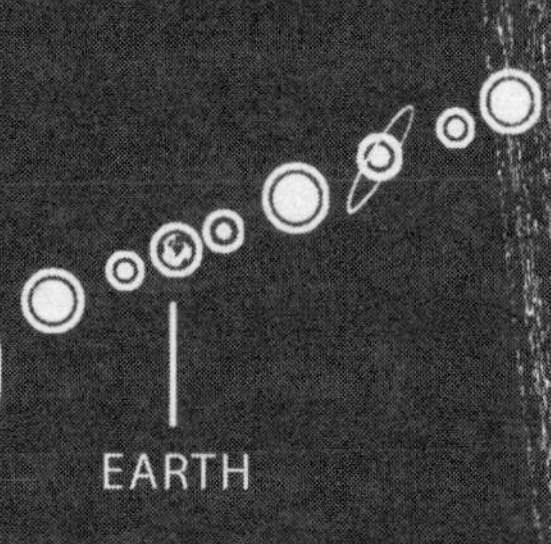

CLAJOXT
GALAXY

JONXTER'S SUN
WESTRENIA'S TWIN MOONS
WESTRENIA
JONXTER GALAXY
Route taken by the *Phoenix*

It is the year 5012 and the Milky Way galaxy is under attack . . .

After the Universal War . . . a war that almost brought about the destruction of every known universe . . . the planets in the Milky Way banded together to create the Intergalactic Force – an elite fighting team sworn to protect and defend the galaxy.

Only the brightest and most promising students are accepted into the Intergalactic Force Academy, and only the very best cadets reach the highest of their ranks and become . . .

To be a Star Fighter is to dedicate your life to one mission: *Peace in Space*. They are given the coolest weapons, the fastest spaceships – and the most dangerous missions. Everyone at the Intergalactic Force Academy wants to be a Star Fighter someday.

Do YOU have what it takes?

Chapter 1

'I'll tell you something interesting,' Anurack said, his four heads bobbing enthusiastically. He held up his fork. 'Something very similar to this green vegetable – which you call a "pea" – grows on Torganora, one of the planets of the Shantanian system in the Crab Nebula. But on that planet it's called a "blarp". That's very interesting, isn't it?' One of his heads looked at Peri, another at Diesel and another at Selene. The fourth just smiled at nothing in particular.

'Erm,' Peri said. 'That's *quite* interesting.'

'Yes, I knew you'd find it interesting,' Anurack said. He popped some chips into the mouth that had just spoken and began speaking from a different head. He was always switching his voice from one head to another. Keeping track of them made Peri dizzy. 'Now, you see this fork? On the planet Sklomp, they don't use forks – they use hollow wooden tubes to suck their food up. Of course, they eat porridge mainly. Isn't that just fascinating?'

Diesel rolled his yellow eyes. Selene snorted, trying to suppress a giggle.

Peri shot her a warning look. It was very important not to offend Anurack: General Pegg, the head of the IF Star Fighters, had told them that Anurack's Galactic Federation were old allies of the Milky Way. The Star Fighters' assignment was simply to return him to his home planet of Koring, keeping him safe and happy. At cruising speed the trip to the Clajoxti galaxy took five days, but there were times when it had seemed more like five months to Peri. Anurack talked non-stop, and was surely the most boring life form in the universe. And that was including the Talking Worms of Betelgeuse.

They had almost reached Koring and were having their last meal together in the *Phoenix*'s restaurant: a classic Earth-style feast of steaks, chips, peas and ketchup, with fruit and ice cream to follow.

'This tomato ketchup,' Anurack said, as he dipped a chip, 'is red, which I believe is the colour of Earthlings' blood. On Jangananx they have a strange superstition that they can't eat anything the colour of their own blood, which is yellow. That means they can't eat bananas. What do you think of that?'

'I think it's really boring,' Diesel muttered.

Oh no! Peri thought. *Diesel's cracked – and we're so close to the end of this endless journey!*

General Pegg had promised the crew of the *Phoenix* that if they carried out this mission on time and without incident, there would be another, much more exciting mission for them. But if they offended Anurack, they'd probably all be grounded indefinitely.

All four of Anurack's heads swivelled in Diesel's direction. One of the heads looked puzzled, one looked suspicious and one looked hurt. The fourth looked all those things at once as it spoke. 'What did you –'

'Diesel said it was really, really *enthralling!*' Peri cut in, with a burst of inspiration.

Anurack's four heads smiled.

'That's it!' Diesel said. 'And very useful. If I ever go to Janganànx, I'll know not to go around offering everyone bananas!'

'Oh, but you could offer them bananas if they were peeled,' Anurack said. 'They love fruit on Janganànx. Do you know, it's been calculated that they eat 5,734 varieties of fruit there?'

Peri stole a look at his watch. They would be docking in fifty-three minutes. Fifty-three long minutes, each filled with sixty long seconds.

'Here we are!' Peri said, fifty-two minutes later. The grey-and-brown sphere of Koring filled the 360-monitor. 'Soon we'll be landing on planet Boring – I mean, *Koring*.'

Selene snorted, just managing to contain her laughter. Diesel had gone and locked himself in his sleeping quarters on Peri's orders because they couldn't risk him upsetting Anurack. Diesel was the spaceship's gunner and much better with weapons than people.

'Koring's a very interesting planet,' Anurack said. 'It orbits our sun at a mean average distance of 121 million kilometres. The atmosphere is composed of 17 different gases . . .'

Peri tuned Anurack out as he concentrated on easing off the boosters and adjusting the Nav-wheel to line the *Phoenix* up with the docking bay below. His special bionic connection with the ship made the tricky move feel simple and instinctive, as though he was manoeuvring his own body into position. Peri's parents were the IF's highest-ranking astronautical engineers, and when they upgraded the legendary spaceship they created a telepathic bond between it and their son. Peri was part bionic and part human, and the *Phoenix* couldn't function without him. A few moments later, it came to rest neatly between the gates of the docking bay.

Peri breathed a sigh of relief. 'Welcome home, Anurack.'

Peri and Selene led Anurack off the Bridge and down a mauve-lit corridor. Peri sent a telepathic order to the *Phoenix* and watched the wall open noiselessly. A ramp extended itself down to the floor of the docking bay, where a group of four-headed Koringers were waiting.

'It's been a pleasant voyage,' Anurack said. 'I've enjoyed talking to you.'

Peri raised his voice to cover Selene's giggle. 'We enjoyed it too.'

'I'll let General Pegg know what a good job you did,' Anurack said. 'I only wish you could come and visit for a little while – I know everything there is to know about Koring, so I could give you a guided tour of the whole planet. You'd find it really interesting.'

'I'm sure we would, but we don't have the time,' Peri said.

He noticed a small timer had appeared in the bottom corner of the Mission Update screen on the control panel. It said, *120 hours, 0 minutes, 0 seconds and 0 tenths of a second.* As he watched, it began to count down, the tenths flickering away at lightning speed, the seconds ticking away steadily after them.

'Well, goodbye, then,' Anurack said.

Peri and Selene waved as Anurack walked down the ramp and the Koringers came forward to greet him.

'Welcome home, Anurack. Did you come back via the Horsehead Nebula?'

'No,' said Anurack, shaking all four of his heads. 'We used the intergalactic highway as far as Rigel, where we turned right on to the hyperspace bypass.'

'You should have gone via the Arcturan Wormhole,' another Koringer said, his heads frowning. There were so many heads now, Peri lost track of who was who. 'That's a quicker way. And there are more interesting things to see . . .'

Peri sent another telepathic order and

the *Phoenix*'s wall closed, blocking the Koringers from view.

Selene punched the air. 'I'm glad that's over!'

Diesel emerged from his quarters. '*S'fâh!* Thank the Spirit of the Universe – Anurack's finally gone!' Diesel kicked his legs in the air for joy. He was half-human, half-Martian, and tended to speak in Martian when he was excited.

There was a faint tap on the *Phoenix*'s wall and it opened silently. Anurack was standing in the entryway.

Diesel, who had his back to the wall, carried on his high-kicking dance, chanting, 'He's gone, gone, *gone*!'

Two of Anurack's heads coughed. Diesel turned around and stopped laughing. His strip of hair turned pink with embarrassment.

There was an awkward silence.

'Erm, Diesel was just . . .' Peri faltered for a moment, before his bionic circuits buzzed with an idea. 'Performing a traditional Martian farewell!'

'I'm acquainted with the customs of Mars,' one of Anurack's heads said, while the other three frowned. 'And I'm not aware of any such dance.'

'We do it all the time,' Diesel said. 'But only when the visitor has left . . . that's why you wouldn't have seen it.'

Three of Anurack's faces smiled. The fourth said, 'Ah, that explains it. An interesting fact to add to my collection! Well, I just forgot my hoverbag.' He beckoned, and the hoverbag rose up and floated along beside him as he exited once more.

Peri closed the wall. 'Let's get out of here before he comes back!'

Soon the *Phoenix* was cruising through outer space.

Peri spoke into the com-system. 'Bridge to Otto – the coast is now clear.'

A section of wall slid open and Otto came slouching on to the Bridge. He had had to hide while Anurack was on board because he wasn't an official member of the team.

He was a former bounty hunter from planet Meigwor, who helped the Star Fighters on their very first mission and never left – but General Pegg could never find *that* out.

'Has he gone?' Otto said. 'It's been really boring staying cooped up in my quarters all this time.'

'Not as boring as being with Anurack!' Selene said.

'What's that?' Otto pointed with his long black tongue at the timer ticking down on the Mission Update screen.

'That's the countdown until our next mission,' Peri explained. 'We have to get back to the IF Space Station before it reaches zero or General Pegg will give our next mission to someone else.'

'Should we go Superluminal?' Diesel asked.

'No need, it's a waste of energy,' Peri said. 'We've got plenty of time, even if we travel at cruising speed.'

'We'd better!' Diesel said. 'I'm looking forward to another mission.'

'I hope I don't have to hide out on this one,' Otto grumbled. 'It's about time I got the chance to use my skills.'

'You haven't got any skills,' Diesel said.

'Oh, really?' Otto boomed. 'Well, let me tell you, you Martian misfit . . .' He hissed and uncoiled one of his long arms, waving it above his head.

Diesel squared up to him, jutting his chin out and clenching his fists.

'Ssshh!' Peri said, holding up his hand. 'What's that noise?'

Strange, low, rhythmic knocking sounds filled the Bridge.

Peri closed his eyes and tuned into the *Phoenix*'s computer. He felt an electric tingling as the noises gradually began to make sense. Peri had never learned Morse code, but the *Phoenix* knew it.

Dot dot dot dash dash dash dot dot dot . . .

'It's an SOS!' Peri said. 'Someone's calling for help!'

Chapter 2

'Where's the SOS coming from?' Selene asked, leaning over the control panel. She was the *Phoenix*'s engineer and knew almost as much about their state-of-the-art spaceship as Peri did, having secretly explored it when she lived on the IF Space Station. She frantically tapped on some keys then straightened up. 'It's being transmitted from an Earth-like planet called Westrenia that orbits a yellow dwarf star in the Jonxter galaxy.'

'Let's see what we can find out about it in *The Space Spotter's Guide*,' Peri said.

Selene tapped some more keys. *The Space Spotter's Guide* appeared on the monitor, followed by *Enter search terms*. She typed in *Westrenia*. Within seconds, images of a blue, green, yellow and orange planet, and its inhabitants, came up. Underneath was an InfoBox:

Westrenia

DESCRIPTION: A medium-sized planet, 11,566 kilometres in diameter. Atmosphere is a mixture of nitrogen, oxygen and trace gases, and is breathable by humans. Has a variety of plant and animal species, including the dominant humanoid species. Westrenia's humanoids are intelligent but their technology is limited. Westrenians only have simple agricultural and manufacturing techniques. Many earn a living by rearing and tending cattle. They recently invented a type of railroad (an early form of mechanised transport – see entry in *The History of Railways*). These humanoids aren't expected to discover interstellar travel for at least another 400 years.

CAUTION: Star Fighters should not interfere with the development of this planet.

RECOMMENDATION: Avoid contact.

'That's impressive!' Peri said. 'Westrenia doesn't have any spaceships, but somehow they've managed to send an SOS into space. We have to go and help them.'

'What are you talking about, you lamizoid?' Diesel said. 'We're not allowed to interfere with less developed species – we learned that in week one at the Academy. It's the most basic IF rule!'

'We also dedicated ourselves to Peace in Space,' Peri said. 'We have to help aliens in need.'

'That would be tough,' Selene said. 'I'm not sure how to help anyone without using my gadgets.'

Diesel's band of hair turned an angry red. 'If we go down in the *Phoenix*, wearing our Expedition Wear, it would totally disrupt their way of life. It would freak out the whole planet!'

'So we'll go in disguise,' Peri said.

'Ridiculous!' Otto said. 'Let's not waste our time helping less developed species. We should get back to the IF base before the clock runs down.'

Peri turned to Selene. 'What do you think?'

'I think it sounds like an adventure!' she said. 'And we can always go Superluminal on the way back if we have to.'

Peri nodded and began to plot a new course. 'Destination: Westrenia!' He watched the stars wheeling around on the 360-monitor as the *Phoenix* changed its direction. 'If we want to help, we'll need to find out more about this planet.'

Four red velvet seats silently rose up from the floor of the Bridge. At the same time, the lights dimmed. The section of wall directly in front of the seats lit up as a pleasant, polite voice came over the speakers: '*Please take your seats. The show is about to commence.*'

'What's going on?' Otto asked suspiciously.

'Don't worry,' Peri said. Through his connection to the *Phoenix*, he could already tell what was about to happen. 'The ship is going to teach us what to expect on Westrenia.'

Peri sat down in one of the red velvet seats. The others sat beside him. *Life in Earth's Old Wild West: A Short Introduction* appeared on the screen in front of them.

'This is cool!' Diesel said. 'It's a pity there's no popcorn.'

A bucket of popcorn instantly materialised by the side of his seat.

'Some sparkling Sirian lushberry juice would be nice,' Selene said.

A cup of sparkling Sirian lushberry juice appeared next to her.

'I wouldn't mind some Meigwor-maggot blood!' Otto said.

Nothing happened.

'This stupid ship hasn't even got any Meigwor-maggot blood!' Otto boomed.

'Sshh!' Peri said. 'Just watch the film.'

An old-fashioned Earth cowboy movie started, with an image of a crowded saloon bar. A man in a waistcoat and a big moustache was pounding a piano in a fast, jazzy style. A group of cowboys played cards at a table with a heap of money in the centre. Suddenly, an

argument broke out. One of the cowboys stood up so abruptly that his chair fell over. He angrily pointed at the player opposite – a man with a beard, a large belly and a checked shirt.

'Why, you low-down, cheatin', yellow-bellied snake,' the first cowboy said. 'You can't have an ace – I got all four aces right here!'

The bearded man stood up, pushing the table aside and swinging a punch at his accuser. Within seconds, everyone at the card table was fighting.

'I hope we don't end up in a bar-room brawl like this on Westrenia,' Peri said to the others.

'That's my kind of place,' Otto said. 'A rough, tough place where arguments are settled with fists!'

'You're totally right!' Diesel said, grinning.

Peri couldn't remember Diesel and Otto ever agreeing about anything before. They looked surprised and slightly embarrassed.

After a short, awkward silence, Diesel said, 'You may be right but you're still ugly.'

Otto flexed his double-jointed arms. 'Shut up, Martian moon-head!'

That sounds a bit more normal, Peri thought.

'We have a problem,' Selene said. 'We're not dressed like those guys in the film.'

'*Undercover Mode engaged,*' the *Phoenix* announced.

The film flicked off. Robotic arms shot out of the ceiling and lifted the Star Fighters up off the floor. Steel arms dressed them in what looked like Expedition Wear but with a hint of the Wild West. The suits clicked and rustled as they tightened to fit. Space-cowboy boots were slipped on to every foot – except Otto's, as his were too big and not really foot-shaped. Peri stretched his legs and heard his metallic spurs clink.

'Cool!' Selene said, adjusting the belt around her waist and checking out her new gear.

'Outstanding!' Peri agreed. The outfit

made him feel tough and adventurous – ready for anything. 'How do I look?'

'Pathetic,' said Diesel. 'Do we really have to wear these old clothes?'

'They aren't really old,' Selene said. She twisted and turned, and the Expedition Wear moved with her.

'What about me?' Otto boomed. 'Do I look like a Westrenian cowboy?'

Peri had to bite his lip not to laugh. Otto's arms were far too long for Expedition Wear – the cuffs ended way above his double-jointed elbows – and the jacket didn't even cover his weapons belt.

Selene gave him a sympathetic look. 'Sorry, Otto. I don't think you'll be able to come on this mission.'

Peri nodded. 'You just wouldn't . . . blend in.'

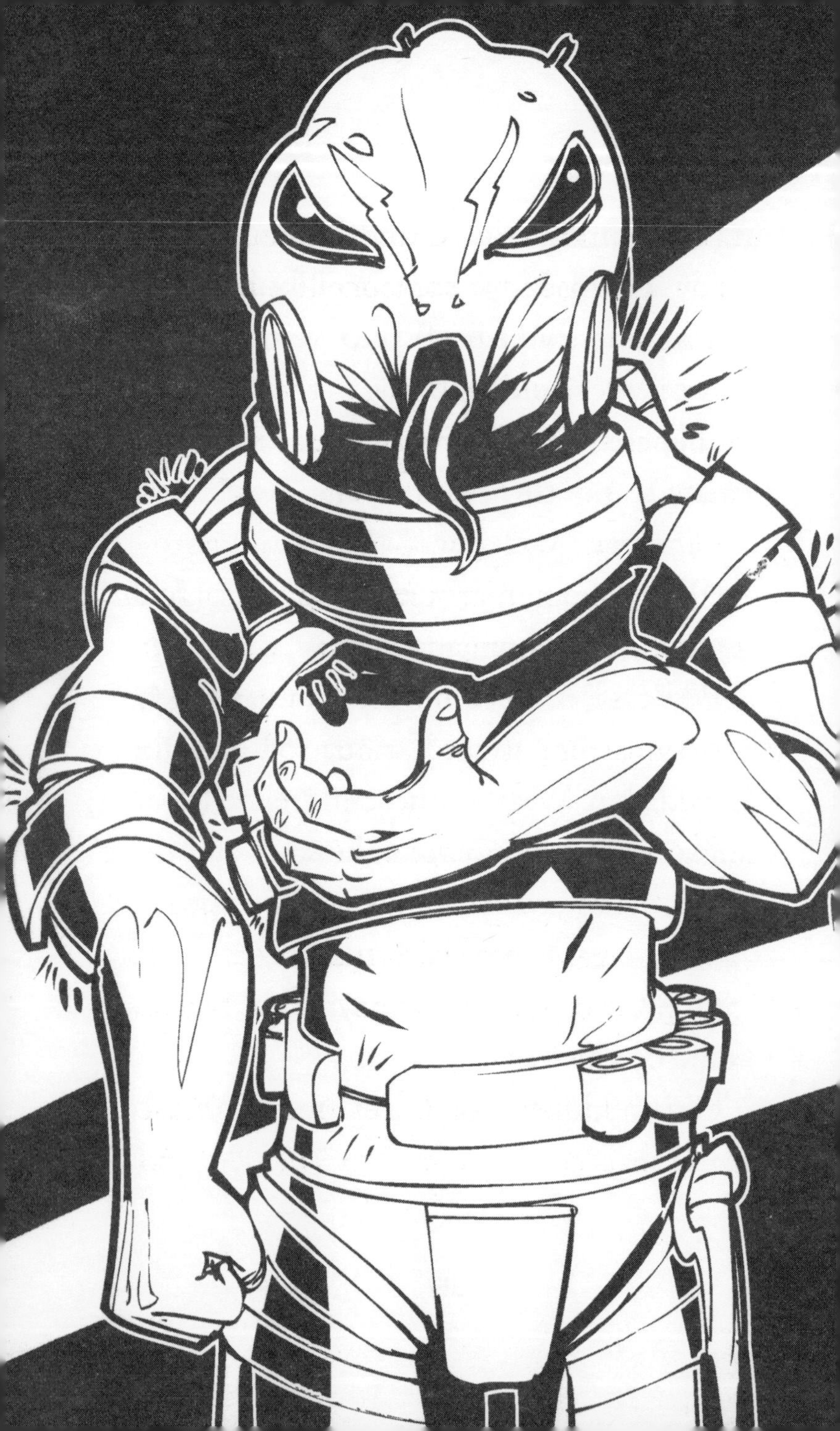

'But it's not fair!' Otto shouted. 'That planet was made for someone like me – all that mindless violence!'

'Entering Westrenia's orbit,' the *Phoenix* announced. *'Take your seats. Final camouflage initiated.'*

The crew sat down and their astro-harnesses snaked around them. Peri felt something digging into his thigh. It was a holster. He removed the weapon. It was quite small and made of purple metal.

'Funny-looking weapon,' he said.

Diesel tutted. 'You couldn't shoot through a spiderweb with that.'

'Don't you boys know anything?' Selene said. 'It's a laser lasso.'

'Oh, right,' Peri said. 'It's one of those ropes that cowboys use to encircle and catch cattle – or enemies. It could come in handy.'

'Yes, but this one's not made of rope,' Selene explained and switched Peri's weapon on.

A sparking fuse of light shot out from the lasso, like a whip.

'*Mh'nak!*' Diesel yelled and snatched the weapon. 'I definitely need one of these.'

'Er, Peri . . .' Selene's voice was a panicked croak. 'Why am I turning green?'

Peri turned around as far as his astro-harness would let him. When he did, he gasped – Selene's skin had definitely changed. It was now a pale, sickly green.

'It's happening to me too!' Diesel said, pointing to his arms. His strip of hair had turned white with fright.

Peri looked down at his own hands,

turning them over and seeing that he had also turned a little bit green. 'It must be the Expedition Wear,' he said. 'It must be configured to make us look like the alien species we're going to encounter on Westrenia.'

'You look like lizard-people!' Otto laughed.

Peri guessed Otto suddenly didn't feel so bad about not getting to explore the alien planet.

Peri turned back to face the 360-monitor. Westrenia now filled the whole screen. It was an Earth-type planet with oceans, ice caps, mountains, forests and large areas of yellow desert and green plains. A pulsing red light showed the location of the SOS signal, coming from what looked like a small town at the edge of a wide desert. Peri beckoned the control panel towards him, initiated the cloaking device and guided the ship down, being careful to keep a safe distance from the settlement. He couldn't let the inhabitants of Westrenia see the *Phoenix*.

The ship touched down gently. The doors opened to reveal a landscape of sand and rocks, with a few tall cactus-like plants growing here and there. In the distance, Peri could see a town and a mountain range behind it.

'Let's go and find the source of that distress signal,' Peri said.

Selene, Peri and Diesel ran down the ramp on to the sand. It felt good to be out in the open after so long aboard the ship.

'I suppose I'll have to stay here with the *Phoenix*,' Otto grumbled from the top of the ramp.

'I don't think that would be safe,' Peri said. 'We can't risk the *Phoenix* being found by someone on this planet. We're going to have to shrink the ship and take it with us.'

'But then I'll be shrunk too!' Otto shouted.

'It won't hurt,' Peri told him.

There was a dial labelled 'Expansion Packs' on the control strip on the wristband of his Expedition Wear. Peri twisted it anticlockwise. The door closed on Otto and, within seconds, the *Phoenix* was the size of a small car . . .

Then the size of a rugby ball . . .

Then the size of an egg.

'That should do it!' Peri said, putting the miniaturised *Phoenix* into his pocket.

Then Peri and his crew set off through the desert towards the town. He could feel it in the excited buzz of his circuits – they were heading for a real adventure.

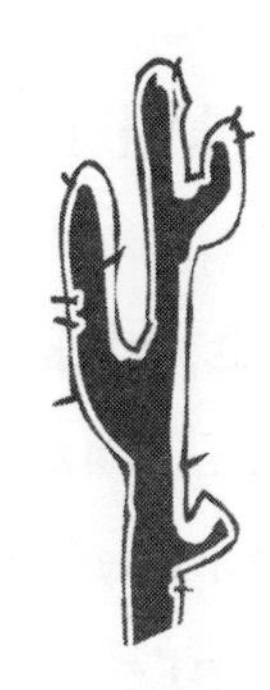

Chapter 3

They soon came to a dirt track that led towards the huddle of buildings they'd seen in the distance. The sun was fierce and Peri felt the sweat trickling down his back.

The sandy, cactus-dotted landscape stretched away as far as their eyes could see. A few whitened cattle-bones lay bleaching in the sun. Peri saw another road that joined the dirt track from the left – it was wide and pitted with wagon-wheel ruts.

'That must be a trade road leading to another town,' he said. 'See those wheel marks? That's where all the stagecoaches have passed along it.'

'I wish we had a stagecoach,' Diesel muttered, wiping blue sweat from his forehead.

'Look,' Selene said. 'There are people working over there.'

A group of aliens, stripped to the waist, were swinging sledgehammers. From here they looked like humans, with the right number of arms and legs, but as the Star Fighters drew closer, Peri saw that their pale green skin was scaly and wrinkly. Their eyes were a deep, dark black. They looked like a cross between a human and an iguana.

They were hammering wooden sleepers into the ground while chanting a song in their alien language.

'They're building a railroad,' Peri said. 'Remember *The Space Spotter's Guide* said that Westrenia has only just invented trains?'

'I wish we had a train,' Diesel grumbled again. 'My feet are killing me.'

'We'd better tune in our SpeakEasies,' Peri said, touching the slight bulge in his neck.

Once the Star Fighters had tuned in to the translator, they were able to understand and speak the aliens' language. After a few moments, Peri heard the words of their chant come into focus. They were singing: 'Hammer, hammer, hammer. Hammer all day. Hammer, hammer, hammer.'

A boring song for a boring job, Peri thought.

'Shall we go and talk to them?' Selene asked.

'I'm not sure,' Peri said. Some instinct was warning him to be cautious. 'Maybe we shouldn't draw attention to ourselves until we've found out a bit more about Westrenia and what's making someone send an SOS.'

'Leave it to me,' Diesel said. As they passed the men, he dipped his head and drawled, 'Howdy, pardners.'

The men broke off their chant. They raised their sweaty faces from their work and stared at him. Nobody spoke. The men's gaze just followed them as the Star Fighters walked on.

'What was that all about?' Diesel said. He touched the bulge in his neck. 'Do you think the SpeakEasy chip couldn't translate "Howdy" into Westrenian?'

'I think they heard you,' Peri said, 'but they didn't want to respond.' He had a feeling that strangers might not be too welcome on Westrenia.

At last the town loomed large ahead of them. They passed a wooden sign that announced: *Buckskinville. Population: 1,032.* They followed the road between two rows of silent wooden houses, all with their blinds down.

They came to a dusty, empty town square. On one side there was a stone well in the shade of a tree, next to a horse trough. Buildings stood all around the square. One of them had a sign over the door that said, *Saloon.* A ball of brown tumbleweed rolled through the square.

'It's quiet,' Diesel said. '*Too* qui—'

The double doors of the saloon bar went

ALOON

flying across the square, spinning and flipping through the air, then hitting the ground and smashing into pieces. Two Westrenian lizard-like men stumbled out of the saloon, fighting. They fell and rolled in the dust, continuing their tussle. Occasionally, they lashed out their lizard-tongues, which made loud, snapping sounds.

I bet those lizard-tongues can do some damage, Peri thought, hoping they wouldn't get into any fights on this strange planet.

'This way,' Peri hissed, dragging Selene and Diesel into a narrow alley. 'Until we know what this is all about, we should stay out of sight.'

A third Westrenian crashed through an upstairs window of the saloon and bounced off the awning below. He was just picking himself up when a fourth jumped through the broken window and sprang off the awning to bundle his foe to the ground. The two of them started slugging it out in the street.

Then a whole crowd of greenish lizard-men tumbled out into the square.

'It's a free-for-all!' Selene said.

'*Ch'açh!*' Diesel said. 'I take that back, about it being too quiet.'

Peri laughed. 'It's a shame Otto can't see this. He'd love – Whoa!' He ducked as a bar stool hurtled through the air and narrowly missed him.

'Do you think we should do something?' Diesel said, watching two furiously struggling bodies roll down the street.

Beside him, Selene dived down as a bottle flew by.

Peri felt a tingle of anxiety in his bionic

belly. 'Why isn't there anyone charging in to arrest them?'

'Maybe they don't have any cops in this town,' Diesel said.

On the other side of the square, Peri spotted a two-storey building with a painted sign hanging outside, displaying a seven-pointed blue star.

'That might be a sheriff's office,' Peri said. 'Come on!' He led them around the edge of the square.

The Star Fighters managed to avoid the flailing fists and feet, the snapping tongues and spinning bottles. Finally, they made it. Peri stepped on to the creaking wooden veranda and pushed open the door.

'Hello?' he called.

No answer.

Peri beckoned to the others, and they

went into the little office. Their boots sounded loud on the wooden floor. There were posters of wanted men on the white-washed walls. Six cells with iron-barred doors stood open and empty. It gave Peri an eerie feeling.

Beyond the six cells was another door.

'Shall we try it?' Peri asked.

'There won't be anyone there,' Diesel said. 'This place is obviously deserted.'

'We'll see,' Selene said. She knocked on the door and turned the handle.

A tall, gangling Westrenian boy was sitting at a desk in the small back office. He was wearing a sheriff's uniform that fit worse than Otto's cowboy outfit. He was hunched over a metal box with a twisted antenna sticking out of it, tapping away at it with some sort of metal instrument. Peri thought it looked like an old-fashioned telegraph and a record player rolled into one.

At the sight of Peri, Selene and Diesel, he leapt to his feet. His hat fell over his deep, black eyes as he groped for his weapon.

Peri and Diesel ran round either side of the desk to grab the boy's arms and keep him from drawing his weapon. His skin felt rough and ridged.

'Easy,' Peri said.

'Get off, you bandits!' shouted the boy. 'You evil outlaws –'

'We're not evil outlaws,' Peri said.

Diesel removed the gun from the boy's holster. When he saw that it was only a wooden toy, he threw it down on the desk. Peri lifted up the boy's hat to see the boy's face staring straight back at him. He was nervous but brave.

'Did Wild Will send you?' the boy demanded.

'Who's Wild Will?' Selene asked. 'We're not from these parts.'

'If you were, you'd know Wild Will. He's the most evil, dangerous bandit in the whole of Westrenia.'

'We're here to help you,' Peri said. 'We heard your distress signal.'

The boy looked with pride at the metal instrument he had been tapping. 'You mean this thing actually worked? Wild Will's gang smashed the machine my father uses to send messages to other towns. I tried to give this one a boost by building an amplifier on the roof. I wasn't sure if it would work at all, let alone send my message as far as the next town. Are you folks from Dry Gulch City?'

'A bit further away than that,' Peri said, sharing a secret smile with Diesel and Selene. They let go of the boy and Peri offered his hand. 'My name's Peri and this is Diesel and Selene.'

'Dexter.' The boy shook hands with all three of them in turn. 'I still can't believe someone heard my message. I hope you don't mind my saying but aren't you a bit . . . *young* to be able to help me?'

'*You* look a bit young to be a sheriff,' Diesel replied.

'My father's the real sheriff. He was kidnapped by Wild Will and his gang.'

'Is that why you were signalling for help?' Selene asked.

Dexter nodded. 'My father, Sheriff Lexor, had finally caught Wild Will and locked him up in this jailhouse, but then Wild Will's gang busted him out and kidnapped my father. No one knows what they've done with him. So the town has no sheriff, which means Wild Will and his gang are in charge. They're unstoppable.'

'No, they're not,' Peri said. 'You've got us now!'

Dexter's story had woken Peri's sense of justice. It just wasn't fair for a villain like Wild Will to bully a whole town into submission. The IF code demanded that the Star Fighters put it right.

'But what can you do?' Dexter asked. 'What can anyone do?'

'If Wild Will has a gang,' Peri said, 'I guess we'll have to get ourselves our own posse.'

Chapter 4

Diesel wiped the sweat from his bedraggled strip of hair. '*Prrrip'chiq!* Westrenia is hotter than that rubbish incinerator on Xion!'

Early the next morning, the Star Fighters had gathered at the junction where the stagecoach road met the dirt track. Already the sun beat down pitilessly and the desert landscape shimmered in the heat haze. They stood in the small patch of shade cast by a giant cactus, which wasn't nearly big enough for all three of them.

'Why did we have to come out here?' Diesel said. 'Why couldn't we stay in town?'

Peri sighed. He'd only explained to Diesel ten times already. 'With Wild Will running Buckskinville, we don't know who we can trust. We need a safe place where we can make our plans in secret.'

'Dexter should be here by now,' Selene said. 'Do you think he's having problems recruiting for our posse?'

'No way, loads of Westrenians will want to join so they can settle their scores,' Peri said, trying to sound confident. 'According to Dexter, the town has been terrorised by Wild Will for ages.'

Peri checked the Mission Update screen on the control strip of his Expedition

Wear: *109 hours, 24 minutes.* Would that be enough time to help Dexter *and* return to the IF Space Station? Peri hoped so.

He scanned the horizon and saw a short line of figures in the distance.

Three of them.

Peri's heart sank to his space-cowboy boots. The two figures alongside Dexter weren't much bigger than the sheriff's son. Peri did his best to put on a brave face.

'Here they come!' he said. 'At least Dexter managed to get a small posse together.'

'Yeah, two kids,' Diesel complained.

'Plus Dexter and us!' Peri said. 'That makes six.'

'How can six of us take on a gang of armed bandits?' Diesel groaned.

Peri looked at Selene for support, but his engineer friend was looking at the ground.

'And it sounds like Wild Will has lots of bandits in his gang,' she said.

'So what?' Peri said. 'We're Star Fighters. We've fought whole armies and survived –'

'But we were in the *Phoenix* then,' Diesel said. 'If we had the *Phoenix* now, Wild Will and his gang wouldn't stand a chance. Without it, *we* don't stand a chance!'

'We didn't have the *Phoenix* when we beat the Xio-Bot,' Peri reminded him. 'And anyway, we're not going to turn our backs on those in trouble!'

Dexter and his two friends had almost reached them now.

Peri waved. 'Howdy!'

'Howdy!' Dexter said. 'These are my friends, Spike and Gunner.'

They were tough, cool-sounding names, but the boys themselves looked neither cool nor tough. Gunner was taller and skinny, with a long neck and high shoulders. Spike was short and squat, with a thatch of bristly red hair under a little white cap. They both looked rather meek and distinctly worried. Their black eyes were wide and their lizard-tongues flicked in and out of their mouths nervously. Gunner's hands seemed to be wrestling with each other, while Spike kept fiddling with his cap, trying to get it to sit right on his bristly hair.

'Good to meet you,' Peri said.

'L-l-likewise,' Gunner said.

'Oh!' Spike's gaze was fixed on Selene. 'I didn't know girls could be in posses.'

Selene glared at him. 'I can fight as well as any boy.'

'Fight?' Gunner said doubtfully. He looked at Dexter. 'But she's a girl!'

'Don't worry about Selene,' Peri said hastily, before Selene proved that she could fight by giving Gunner a blacker eye than he already had. 'We've been in plenty of scrapes together and she can look after herself, I promise you. We just have to work out our first move against Wild Will and his gang.'

'Are we really going to atta-atta-attack him?' asked Spike.

'Yes, but not head-on,' Peri said. 'That wouldn't be smart. We're outnumbered and outgunned.'

'You got that right,' Gunner said. 'Wild Will's gang have all the weapons in town.'

Peri nodded. 'Right, but do you know what their strongest weapon is?'

'Wild Will's spring-loaded repeating rifle,' Dexter said.

'That rifle does sound deadly, but that wasn't what I meant,' Peri said. 'Their strongest weapon is *fear*. The townsfolk are too scared to stand up to Wild Will. If we can stop them being scared –'

'How can we do that?' demanded Gunner.

Diesel and Selene looked at Peri inquisitively. 'I'd be kind of curious to know that too,' Diesel said.

'We have to stand up to the gang,' Peri said. 'We'll see how tough they really are when the townsfolk aren't scared of them.'

'But the townsfolk *are* scared,' Gunner said. He turned, flicked his tongue out and spat.

To Peri's amazement, a globule of spittle travelled a huge distance, flying right across the road, hitting a cactus and making it wobble.

'Wow – that was some spit, Gunner!' Peri said.

Gunner shrugged. 'I've spat farther.'

'Let's get down to business!' Diesel said impatiently. 'What's the plan?'

'We should spend some time training these boys to fight,' Peri said.

'We don't have long,' Diesel said. 'The clock's ticking down, remember?'

Diesel was right. Peri glanced at his Expedition Wear control strip again.

'That's the fanciest watch I've ever seen,' Dexter said.

'Don't worry about that,' Peri said. 'We need to start training – and fast! Now, did you boys manage to get hold of anything that could be used as a weapon?'

'Yeah,' Dexter said.

From under their shirts, Dexter, Spike and Gunner pulled out the strangest-looking objects Peri had ever seen.

'M-m-made them ourselves,' Spike said.

The Star Fighters looked at the strange tubes for a moment, then at each other.

Peri grinned. 'I think this might just work.'

Chapter 5

'You can do this, Spike,' said Peri.

The smaller of Dexter's two friends was turning green – greener than he was in the first place. Selene's chokehold on Spike was tight. Peri feared that the little Westrenian boy might pass out before he managed to escape.

Peri had structured their day's training carefully. First up was spit practice. Using their special, spiralled tubes, Dexter, Spike and Gunner spat stones across the desert, hitting every cactus they targeted. Gunner even hit one that was hundreds of metres away. Once their confidence was higher, Peri had them run escape drills, like the ones taught at the IF Academy. He and Diesel tackled or restrained the Westrenians, who dodged, jumped and wriggled free. Peri thought it was also a great refresher course for the Star Fighters. He realised he relied too much on the *Phoenix* and his bionic abilities. It was good to get back to the basics. These Westrenian boys were demonstrating that smartness, skills and confidence might just outwit outlaws and their weapons.

The last escape drill involved Selene applying the kind of chokehold that Diesel predicted bandits like Wild Will and his gang would use, and it was up to the

Westrenian boys to escape. They struggled at first but, after a couple of hours, they were able to slip out of Selene's grasp, sometimes even throwing her to the sand. Except for Spike, whose little legs had come right off the ground and whose little white cap had flown off. He kicked desperately, trying to get free, but Selene held on tight.

'You can do this, Spike!' Peri said again.

He saw the little alien's black eyes narrow for just a moment, his lizard-tongue flicking out in determination. With a growl, he bent forward and threw Selene to the sand.

'Ouch!' the engineer cried.

'Well done, Spike!' Gunner said, slapping his friend on the back.

'That was great!' Peri said. 'If any of Wild Will's men grab you, that's how you should escape.'

'I think I've got it,' Spike said, reaching down to help Selene to her feet.

'Good moves,' Selene said with a smile. 'You'll be a match for anyone.'

Spike ran a hand over his bristly red hair, his black eyes dropping shyly. 'I hope you weren't letting me get the better of you, Miss Selene.'

'That's not her style,' Peri said, giving her a playful punch in the arm. 'Trust me.'

'Selene hates losing more than Otto hates vegetables,' Diesel agreed.

Dexter cocked his head questioningly. 'What are vegetables?'

'And who is Otto?' asked Gunner.

The Star Fighters glanced at each other, then Peri shook his head.

'That doesn't matter,' Peri said. 'All that matters is that we're ready.'

'I feel ready,' said Gunner.

'Me too,' Spike said, shoving his cap on his head.

Peri turned to the sheriff's son. 'Dexter?'

Dexter grinned and half turned, lashing his tongue out and sending a globule of spit zooming towards an old, withering cactus tree. It took the tip off one of the branches. Peri watched, amazed, as the broken chunk of prickly cactus hit the ground and broke into pieces.

'Oh yes,' said Dexter. 'I think I'm ready.'

'That's just as well,' Diesel said, stomping around impatiently in his cowboy boots. 'Because . . . look!'

Peri followed Diesel's pointed finger and saw a narrow dirt road that skirted the desert. Far down the road, on the horizon, a cloud of dust was rising. It was getting closer. Peri's bionic eyes zoomed in on ten figures that were galloping towards them.

I bet they're Wild Will's men, he thought.

Peri was right – and they were heading straight for a herd of animals that were being shepherded by a small group of Westrenians, their lizard-tongues snapping in the air to encourage the animals to move faster. The animals were short, squat and four-legged. They looked like the cattle on planet Earth, except their skin was green with deep-red spots.

'Hide!' Peri instructed.

His new team obeyed instantly. Diesel and Selene dropped to the ground, while Peri and the Westrenian boys dived behind cacti and scrubby bushes.

Riding strange, horse-like creatures, Wild Will's gang drew up alongside the herd, whooping and jeering.

'Stop, or you'll regret it!' one of the bandits shouted.

Panicking, the cattle-drivers yelled at their animals, desperately trying to control them. Most of the cattle-creatures stopped, but a few made frightened, screeching sounds and trotted off in all directions as fast as their stumpy legs would carry them.

'Should we do something?' Diesel asked as he crawled on his belly to where the others were hiding.

'We can't let them steal the cattle,' Gunner said, making to start forward.

'Wait,' Peri said, putting a hand on the Westrenian's shoulder and pulling him back behind a prickly cactus. 'I don't think they're stealing anything.'

Selene agreed. 'They're just scaring the cattle-drivers.'

The Star Fighters' posse watched as Wild Will's bandits fired their weapons in the air, spooking the cattle and causing them to stampede. Then the bandits wheeled their horses around and began riding away, shouting and laughing at the workers.

'What did they do that for?' Dexter asked, his tongue slithering over his lips.

Peri could tell the boy was furious.

'To show the townsfolk that they can push around anybody they want to,' Peri said.

Diesel growled. 'They're just bullies.'

'Too right,' Peri said. 'And the one thing no bully can handle is someone standing up to them. Come on.'

With that, he led the others off at a fast jog along a dry ditch, back towards Buckskinville. It was time for the Star Fighters – and their posse – to try to save the town.

Chapter 6

The first thing the new posse saw when they returned to the square in Buckskinville was what appeared to be several horses tethered at the trough. But on closer inspection, although these animals looked a bit like Earth horses, they had leathery hides instead of glossy coats, and a ridge of sharp spikes running down their necks instead of a mane. Apart from the Westrenian horses' soft stamps and occasional neighs, it was dead quiet.

'What are we going to do?' Dexter asked.

'I'm going to talk to the townsfolk,' Peri said. 'I need to let them know we're here to help, and that together we can defeat Wild Will's gang.'

'Yeah, but the gang's already back,' Dexter said, pointing at the horses. 'Are you sure it's a good idea?'

'It's a risk,' Selene said. 'But the only way we'll beat Wild Will and his men is if the whole town stands up to them!'

'That's right,' Peri said. He walked right into the centre of the square, cleared his throat and shouted in a loud, ringing voice, 'People of Buckskinville! I'm a stranger to these parts – I come from far away.' *That's an understatement,* Peri thought. 'And me and my friends are here to help and to tell you that you don't need to fear Wild Will and his gang any more. Wild Will's men may seem tough, but that's only because they've convinced you to be afraid of them. If we stand up for ourselves, then we can beat them! But we must work together.'

Around the square, a few windows and doors creaked open. Several men, women and children poked their heads out cautiously. Peri looked at their faces in turn, addressing them directly.

'I can understand why you might not want to take the word of a stranger,' he said. 'You don't know me or my friends. But you *do* know Dexter, Spike and Gunner.'

The three Westrenian boys all nodded, grinning bashfully.

'If you stand up to these outlaws,' Peri said, 'you can drive them right out of your town!'

'There's just one tiny problem,' said a man from an upstairs window. He had glasses over his dark eyes, and his lizard-tongue wiped sweat from his bald, scaly brow. 'How can we stand up to these outlaws when we don't have a sheriff and we don't have weapons?'

'Remember that they're just cowardly bullies!' Peri said. 'You've already got the advantage of numbers on your side – you just need to believe in yourselves and then you'll be a force to be reckoned with.'

A loud, slow clapping broke out. Peri turned round to see a large, tall Westrenian standing in the doorway of the saloon. He was wearing a black cowboy hat. Below the brim, Peri could see that his thin lips were curled into a smirk and a frill of scales fanned out from his neck.

At his waist was a belt in which six guns were holstered. A rifle was slung over his shoulder. His sleeves were rolled up and Peri saw that his scaly arms were covered in red tattoos of skulls, severed heads and dripping knives.

All the townsfolk had ducked back behind their doors and windows.

Wild Will, Peri thought.

The applause got louder. More outlaws appeared at every side and corner of the square, clapping along with their leader.

'That was one fine speech, boy!' Wild Will said, his voice a slithering rasp. 'You should run for mayor when you grow up – if you get the chance to grow up, that is!'

The bandits laughed.

Peri realised that they were in big trouble. They were surrounded, and the bandits were all armed. The townsfolk were still too afraid to help. Somehow Peri and his posse had to get out of there.

'So,' Wild Will said, pointing a finger at Peri, 'it seems you and your friends are putting together a gang of your own. Remember, young Dexter, I still have your father. Do you want him to suffer more than he already has?'

Peri was barely listening to Wild Will now. His eyes were desperately searching the square, hoping for a flash of inspiration.

Then it came.

He spoke softly to Selene and Diesel. 'The horses.'

Diesel looked confused, but Selene's face brightened in understanding. She pulled Diesel to her side. Peri moved closer to Wild Will to draw his attention as Selene and Diesel slowly sidestepped to where the horse-creatures were tethered.

'You're the ones who should be worried!' Peri said loudly, to distract from Selene and Diesel. 'And as long as you keep harassing the townsfolk, we'll keep getting in your way!'

Wild Will laughed, and so did his men. 'Well, you're going to have your work cut out! We're not going to stop taking what we want. In fact, we're going to rob every stagecoach that passes by this town, and we're going to get rich and then we're going to use our riches to open up mines on the edge of town.' He raised his voice. 'Legend says there's gold beneath Buckskinville. We intend to find it.' He paused and spoke even louder. 'We'll get rich – and so will everyone else in this town!'

So that's how Wild Will keeps the townsfolk in line, Peri thought. *It's not just fear – it's the promise of reward as well. But don't they see? If Wild Will opens up the mines, he'll turn them all into his slaves!*

'Anyone who tries to stop us will regret it, won't they, boys?'

'Yes, boss!' the bandits chanted. They raised their guns and pointed them at Peri, Dexter, Spike and Gunner.

'Whoa there!' Wild Will said. 'Don't shoot them – that would be too easy! We should make an example of them – show the good people of Buckskinville what happens when you cross Wild Will!'

The outlaws reholstered their guns and began to close in on the new posse from all

sides of the square, their black eyes boring into them.

Selene gave a low whistle. Peri looked round and saw that the horses had been untethered.

'Run!' he said, and led Dexter and his two friends in a sprint to the horse trough.

'Stop them!' shouted Wild Will.

The bandits rushed towards the horses,

but Peri got there first and leapt on to one. Selene and Diesel had already mounted two of them. They slapped the sides of the remaining horses, which started running towards Dexter, Spike and Gunner. The three Westrenian boys jumped on to the saddles with ease as they galloped by.

Wild Will's gang lunged at the horses.

Out of the corner of his eye, Peri saw Selene twisting in her saddle to avoid the lashing tongue of a bandit.

Dexter, Gunner and Spike, all experienced riders, skilfully dodged the bandits. Diesel was bringing up the rear and none of Wild Will's posse had managed to stop him either.

Peri felt a jolt of pressure at his ankle and struggled to stay in his saddle. He looked down and saw that a thin, pink tongue had coiled itself around his leg. He followed the trail of the tongue to see a big Westrenian bandit tugging at his leg.

Peri felt a surge of fury and he kicked out with all his super strength, feeling the tongue loosen its hold. *Thwack!* It whipped back on itself and hit the alien in the face, sending him tumbling over into the dust.

'We made it!' Peri shouted, as the six of them rode out of the square.

'Use your lassos, boys!' Wild Will yelled.

Whoooosh! Peri ducked as a lasso skimmed over his head. It was a close one.

'Ouch!'

To his left, Peri saw that Diesel had been snared by another lasso. The half-Martian gave a startled cry as he was yanked out of the saddle. *'Prrrip'chiq!'*

'Diesel!' shouted Selene.

Peri steered his horse around. Diesel was already being dragged back by Wild Will, who held the other end of the lasso. Peri was faced with a difficult decision and felt as if he was being torn in two. They had to rescue Diesel, but if they turned around now, they'd all be caught and the people of

Buckskinville would have no hope of defeating Wild Will.

'We'll be back for you, Diesel!' shouted Peri. 'I promise!'

But when and how? he asked himself.

Chapter 7

Peri held Dexter's telescope up to his eye. He saw some of Wild Will's men skulking about the alleys or brandishing their pistols threateningly. Others went round the town square tacking up hastily drawn posters on tree trunks and walls. He turned the eyepiece of the telescope to bring one into focus. It showed a big-nosed boy with crooked eyes. Peri could just make it out:

WANTED DEAD OR ALIVE
(PREFERABLY DEAD):
notorious, troublemaking kid who
ain't from round these parts.
Reward: 100 zorns.

Peri lowered the telescope. 'Those bandits can't draw to save their lives – that looks nothing like me!'

It was late in the afternoon. Peri checked the countdown. Now they had only 97 hours and 24 minutes to rescue Diesel and the sheriff, save the town and return to the

IF Space Station! Their situation seemed to be getting worse.

They had left the horses tethered underneath a tree and had sneaked closer to Buckskinville. They were lying on their stomachs on a small hill just outside town.

'Let me see,' Dexter said, taking the telescope from Peri. He scanned the square. 'There are *lots* of posters up. We've all got a price on our heads!'

'Can I see?' asked Selene. She looked through the telescope – and started. 'Oh, Rigel rats!'

'What is it?' Peri said.

Selene handed him the telescope. 'Look at the far end of the square,' she said grimly.

Through the round lens, Peri saw that Diesel and a man who he guessed was Dexter's father were being pulled along at the end of a rope by the bandits. Wild Will was standing by a strange patch of dark earth. Diesel and the sheriff were brought right up to its edge, then Wild Will jabbed each of them in the back with his tongue. They fell forward into the dark patch – and disappeared.

For a moment Peri was bewildered. 'I just saw Diesel and your dad, but I think they've been pushed down a hole!' he said.

Dexter took the telescope from him. He peered through it and groaned. 'It's the Hole of Death!'

'What's that?' Peri asked. 'It doesn't sound good.'

Dexter didn't seem able to speak.

Gunner answered for him. 'It's a form of punishment. They throw prisoners down a hole that's too deep to climb out of. There's

no food, no water and no protection against the sun. They're left there to die.'

Peri looked through the telescope again. He saw Wild Will and his men walking away, laughing.

'We have to get our friends out of there!' Peri said.

They sat around a campfire that Spike and Gunner had made on the other side of the hill, out of sight of the town. The sky had darkened and silver stars twinkled over Westrenia. Another time, Peri might have enjoyed the strange sight of the two round golden moons hanging in the sky. But now his only thought was: *How are we going to get Dexter's father and Diesel out of the Hole of Death?*

'I suppose it's no good hoping the townsfolk will set them free?' Selene asked.

Dexter shook his head. 'They're too scared of ending up in the Hole themselves.'

'And there are too many of Wild Will's men guarding it for us to attack,' Spike said.

'If they weren't all there together, we'd have a chance,' Peri said thoughtfully. 'Now, what would make a large group of the bandits leave the town?'

'Something they can rob,' Selene said. 'Like a stagecoach!'

'Didn't Wild Will say they would rob every coach that passed?' Gunner asked.

'The mail coach goes by tomorrow morning,' Dexter said. 'They'll have their eye on that, I'm certain!'

Peri smacked his fist into the palm of his hand. 'Then that's when we'll strike!'

*

In the distance, a coyote howled up at the two moons. It was cold – the desert temperature dropped dramatically at night. Peri shivered as he tossed and turned under the saddlecloth he was using for a blanket. The others had already managed to drift off to sleep, but Peri's bionic systems were buzzing, keeping him awake.

He kept running over tomorrow in his mind, imagining different possibilities. It would make things easy if Wild Will's whole gang went to rob the mail coach, but that wasn't very likely. Some men would surely stay behind to guard the Hole of Death. Wild Will might even stay behind.

Peri decided that his own posse would have to split up. If the others could thwart the mail coach robbers, he would try to take care of Wild Will alone. He only hoped his laser lasso and bionic abilities would be a match for Wild Will's spring-loaded repeating rifle.

He turned again and felt something pushing into his hip. For a moment he wondered what it could be. He dug his hand into the pocket of his Expedition Wear and pulled out . . . the *Phoenix*!

He had almost forgotten about it. The twin moons cast a yellow light on it as he held the most advanced spaceship ever built in the palm of his hand. The *Phoenix*'s door slid open and out walked the teeny-tiny, bug-sized figure of Otto, shaking his fist and squeaking. His voice was so high-pitched that Peri couldn't make out the words.

He tuned into his special connection with the *Phoenix*, imagining that he had shrunk along with it. Otto's voice seemed to lower in pitch and Peri was able to understand him.

'. . . been shaken about all over the place! I had to strap myself into bed or I would've been smashed to pieces! What have you been doing? Trampolining?'

Peri thought back over events since they landed on Westrenia. He'd trained the posse in fighting skills, jumped in and out of ditches, and escaped alien bandits by galloping on a horse. It must have been a rough ride for poor Otto!

'Sorry,' Peri whispered. 'It's been a bit crazy here.'

'How much longer is this going on for? I'm getting space-sick!'

'It'll be over tomorrow,' Peri whispered. He was anxious not to wake the others. 'I hope.'

'You do realise that won't give us much time to get back to the Space Station?' Even in his miniature form, Otto had a booming voice.

'It'll be all right,' Peri said. 'We'll make it.'

'Who are you talking to, Peri?' said a sleepy voice. Dexter had woken up!

Peri's first thought was to jam the *Phoenix* back in his pocket, but the door was still open and Otto might fall out or get squished. Before Peri could act, Dexter had crawled over and crouched beside him.

'What's that? Some kind of egg with a squeaking insect inside?' Dexter asked.

'Er, yes, sort of,' Peri said.

Otto started squeaking curses in Meigwor.

Dexter leaned forward to get a closer look. 'That's not an insect!' he gasped. 'It's a tiny, little, red man, with an extra-long neck and arms, and – he's wearing clothes!' Dexter pinched his own arm. 'Ouch! I'm not dreaming! Peri, what is that thing? You must know, because you talked to it.'

'We-e-ell . . .' Peri began. But no convincing story came to mind. It was against IF rules to tell the Westrenians about the advanced technology of other civilisations, but Dexter was his friend and deserved to know the truth. 'It's a kind of ship for travelling to other planets and stars,' Peri said. 'We call it a "spaceship". And the little man is an alien from a planet called Meigwor.'

'Hey, you're joshing me!' Dexter said. 'You can't travel in that thing. It's way too small!'

'It's been shrunk right now, but it can be enlarged,' Peri explained. 'Watch.'

He gave a slight clockwise twist to the 'Expansion Packs' dial on the control strip. The ship ballooned until it was as big as an ostrich egg and Otto was about the size of a bee.

Dexter's eyes bulged like Venusian gooseberries. 'Astonishing! And how big can it get?'

'It can grow to the size of a planet,' Peri said, enjoying the utter amazement on Dexter's face.

'And you travel to other stars and planets in it?'

Peri nodded. 'We were in outer space when your distress signal came through.'

Dexter started to laugh. 'I knew you weren't from around here, but I never thought anything could be *that* far away! All my life I've wanted something magic – something plain impossible – to happen. And now it has!'

'Yes,' Peri said. 'But you mustn't tell anyone. Not even Spike and Gunner. It's supposed to be a secret.'

Dexter put his hand over his heart. 'I won't say a word. But tell me, has this spaceship of yours got weapons?'

'Space Cannon, lasers and loads more,' Peri said. 'I doubt my crew and I have even discovered half of its capabilities.'

'Can't we use them to blast Wild Will and his gang out of town?'

Peri shook his head. 'We're not allowed to use our weapons on Westrenia. That's against Intergalactic Force rules. All planets must be allowed to develop at their own rate. If your planet discovered life on other planets that's much more technologically advanced, it could interfere with your development. So we have to beat Wild Will using only this planet's technology.'

'We *will* beat him though,' Dexter said. 'Since you're from beyond the stars, I bet you're super-smart, right? Wild Will doesn't stand a chance against you and your pals!'

'You have to help too,' Peri said. 'We

won't win without you and Spike and Gunner.'

Peri shrank the *Phoenix* back to egg size, closed the door on the still squeaking Otto and slipped the ship back in his pocket.

'Time to get some sleep,' he said. 'We need all the energy we can get if we're going to do battle with the outlaws tomorrow. Goodnight, Dexter.'

'Goodnight, spaceman!'

A few minutes later, Dexter was fast asleep. But sleep was a long time coming to Peri. He hoped he'd be able to keep his word to Dexter. Beating Wild Will wasn't going to be easy. Peri hoped they could beat him quickly too. Because, if everything went as planned, the Star Fighters would have just three days to make it home.

Chapter 8

The Westrenian sun was climbing in the sky. It was getting hot already. Spike and Gunner had sneaked into town early that morning to grab the final supplies they needed for their plan. Now Peri and the posse crouched in a ditch, waiting for the mail coach. Selene had some firecrackers and a coil of rope. Every now and then, Dexter shot a brief smile at Peri as if to say, *Your secret's safe with me.*

'Does everyone know what they're doing?' Peri asked.

Selene nodded.

The Westrenians fingered their spiral spitball pipes in anticipation and all gave a thumbs-down sign.

'What?' Peri said. 'You *don't* know what you're doing?'

'Sure we know,' Spike said, giving the thumbs-down sign again.

'Then why –' Peri began, but Selene interrupted him.

'Here comes the coach!'

Peri saw it on the horizon, racing along in a cloud of dust. He made out four armed men on the roof, as well as two riders galloping alongside. Clearly, news of Wild Will's gang had spread, and the mail coach company wasn't taking any chances in his territory. That was a good sign – it meant there would be even more of them to fight the outlaws. *We need them,* Peri thought.

He looked towards town and saw Wild Will's men advancing. He quickly counted that there were twenty riders. *Wild Will must have sent almost the whole gang!* Even with the extra mail coach guards, the Star Fighters' posse was going to be heavily outnumbered.

'I'm heading into town,' Peri said. 'You sort out these guys, and I'll take down Wild Will and rescue Diesel and the sheriff – OK?'

'Good luck, Peri!' Selene said.

Gunner grinned and gave a thumbs-down sign.

Oh, right, Peri realised. *Thumbs down is a* good *sign on Westrenia!* It felt strange, but he returned the thumbs-down sign. Then he set off, running along the ditch as fast as he could and keeping his head down.

Soon he heard shouting and gunfire behind him. He forced himself to keep running without looking back.

When Peri got near the town, he checked over the top of the ditch, then jumped out of it.

One of Wild Will's gang was standing by the Buckskinville town sign. The alien was leaning on a rifle. *A lookout,* Peri thought.

The alien's lizard-tongue ran over his lips and cheek. Peri had to get past him somehow. He felt an electric tingling in his chest which spread to his arms and legs. His bionic powers were kicking in. He decided not to bother with anything too subtle. He didn't have much time.

He ran straight towards the Westrenian at superhuman Fight-or-Flight speed.

'What?' Startled, the outlaw picked up his rifle and took aim.

Peri zigzagged around the bullets that whizzed towards him. Nanoseconds later, he had reached the bandit. Peri gave a bionic kick to one of the tottery wooden legs that held up the Buckskinville sign. The wooden board crashed down on to the bandit's head. He collapsed in the dust, out for the count.

Peri ran into town, staying as low as he could in case the townsfolk were keeping a lookout on Wild Will's orders.

He quickly made his way to the far end of the town square, where he found the Hole of Death. It smelt pretty bad: a horrible mix of sweat, mud and rubbish that the bandits had thrown in. Flies hovered above the hole, buzzing hungrily. Diesel and the sheriff looked up at him. Up close, Peri could see the sheriff's resemblance to Dexter – they shared the same fair hair and the same square, determined jaw.

'About time!' Diesel said. 'I'm parched and I'm starving!'

'I got here as fast as I could!' Peri said. 'I'll get you out after I've dealt with Wild Will.'

'Be careful, lad,' said the sheriff. 'He's more dangerous than you might think!'

'Don't worry about me,' Peri said. Then he straightened up and walked into the centre of the square. 'Wild Will!' he shouted. 'Where are you hiding, you coward?'

Heads popped out from upstairs windows as there was a crash from within the saloon.

Wild Will stood on the step, a cigar in his mouth. His frill of scales fanned out from his neck, making his head look three times its normal size. His lizard-grin made Peri uneasy.

'Well, what have we here? Aren't you the boy on one of those Wanted posters? I could do with that hundred zorn reward. Now, the poster says, "Dead or alive", but I don't think I'll bother with "alive". Dead prisoners are much easier to control.'

Wild Will slid his rifle from his shoulder and clicked off the safety catch. Before he could take aim, Peri whipped out his laser lasso and flicked it on. The glowing laser rope flew out and coiled round the barrel of Wild Will's rifle.

Wild Will's shot blasted harmlessly into

the sky, scaring the birds from a tree at the edge of the square.

Peri tugged, trying to jerk the rifle from Wild Will's grasp, but the outlaw held on tight. Peri felt the strength of his resistance. Wild Will was heavy and powerful – he wouldn't let go unless he had to. The alien outlaw threw back his head and darted his tongue at the laser lasso, trying to break Peri's hold. Peri switched off the device's power. This caught Wild Will by surprise, causing him to stumble backward and crash into the wooden rail outside the saloon.

There was a murmur from the watching townsfolk – and Peri was sure he heard laughter.

Wild Will was getting to his feet. 'Why, you little –'

'Listen,' Peri said, 'why don't we settle

this once and for all? How about a good, old-fashioned duel? Let's see who's fastest on the draw.'

Wild Will began to raise his rifle again. 'No, I'd prefer just to shoot you down in cold blood!'

'What's the matter, Wild Will?' called a voice from one of the houses. 'Scared you'll lose to a boy?'

There was an excited mutter from the watching crowd. More lizard-heads were appearing at windows and peeping round corners.

Wild Will laughed harshly. 'I'm the fastest draw in these here parts. The graveyards are filled with the bones of those who have challenged me and lost. A kid like him doesn't stand a chance. He doesn't even have a weapon!'

'I have this,' Peri said, brandishing his laser lasso.

'All right, then!' Wild Will said. 'Let's see if you think your fancy-dan lasso can help you against a pistol.' A look of cunning came over the outlaw's face. He began to walk back towards the saloon. 'Guess I won't need my rifle. I'll just put it in here for safe keeping. My six-shooter should take care of you just fine. Wait there, boy – don't you run away!'

'Running away isn't my style,' Peri said, squaring his shoulders.

Wild Will went up the step and disappeared into the saloon. He was gone a little longer than Peri had expected. While he waited, Peri looked at the faces watching him through the windows around the square. Several smiled encouragingly. Others gave the thumbs-down sign. He heard someone whisper, 'Good luck, stranger boy!'

The sun was directly overhead now. Peri's shadow was a small black blob at his feet.

It was high noon.

Wild Will reappeared from the saloon, without his rifle. He strode into the square, hands hanging by his scaly sides. He stopped and stared at Peri. A wide stretch of dusty ground lay between them. Peri calculated that his laser lasso would just about reach the alien outlaw.

'You know the rules, boy?' Wild Will asked. 'Keep your weapon in its holster. I'm gonna count to three, then we'll see who's fastest on the draw!'

Peri nodded. He felt a tingling in his chest.

Wild Will cleared his throat. 'One . . .'

Peri watched the bandit's hands carefully. He wouldn't put it past Wild Will to draw and shoot before the count was completed.

'Two . . .'

Peri caught a tiny movement out of the corner of his eye. He glanced and saw the barrel of a rifle poking through the shuttered window of the saloon.

It was pointing straight at him!

Chapter 9

The tingling in Peri's chest spread to his arms and legs as his bionic powers took hold again. He threw himself to the ground just as Wild Will said, 'Three!'

The rifle in the window fired.

The bullet passed over Peri's head and thudded into a building on the far side of the square. Peri rolled, feeling dust spray his face. A bullet from Wild Will's six-shooter had struck the exact position where Peri had been lying just a second before.

He saw sunlight glint off the rifle barrel. *It's tracking me!*

Fighting out in the open was very different to firing weapons from the Bridge of the *Phoenix*. Peri knew he was going to need all his super strength and bionic speed to survive an attack from two armed, alien outlaws.

From his position on the ground, Peri drew his laser lasso and whipped it towards the window. The loop settled and tightened around the rifle barrel and jerked it to the side just before it fired again.

The bullet zipped past Wild Will's ear, making him jump and upsetting his aim. Wild Will's shot went skywards.

Using his Fight-or-Flight speed, Peri

jumped up and ran, holding his laser lasso tight. He pulled the rifle clean through the saloon window, dragging one of Wild Will's bandits out with it. There were cheers and laughter from the watching townsfolk as the bandit crashed to the ground.

Peri threw himself to one side, feeling the rush of air as a bullet from Wild Will's six-shooter zoomed past his arm, only narrowly missing him. It splintered a veranda rail. Peri ran at bionic speed across the square.

Wild Will had drawn a second pistol now. Bullets followed Peri, ricocheting off the fronts of the houses.

Peri made it to the edge of the square and dived behind the stone well just as another bullet rebounded off the side.

'Come out and fight, you little coward!' Wild Will snarled.

'*You*'re the coward!' Peri shouted back. 'You cheated!'

'It's true!' shouted a man who was leaning out from an upstairs window. Peri chanced a look around the square and saw that it was the same bald man, with the timid expression, who had called out yesterday. Only he didn't look so timid now. 'Wild Will *did* cheat. He got Stinky Stan to snipe at the boy – because he knew he couldn't beat him fair and square!'

There were shouts of agreement from the onlookers.

Wild Will raised his gun and the bald man hastily withdrew from sight.

'I'm going to teach all you folks a lesson!' Wild Will bellowed, his tongue snapping angrily at the air. 'I'm going to make sure I get the respect I deserve from this one-horse town – right after I finish with this pesky kid!'

Wild Will continued marching towards the well, both guns at the ready. Peri could just see him by peeking round the side of the well – if he leaned out further to fire his laser lasso, he'd be giving his enemy a clear shot.

Peri snatched a rock from the crumbling well and threw it out, far away from where he was crouching.

Wild Will spun round and shattered the rock with one well-placed bullet. Peri took his opportunity, darting out from the other side of the well. He saw Wild Will spin back, pistols aimed, but Peri was too fast. A loop of laser rope shot out and wrapped around Wild Will's body, pinning his arms to his sides. His guns pointed harmlessly down at the ground.

The outlaw struggled furiously, his scales turning a darker green as he did so. He hissed and viciously flicked his tongue at Peri. The harder he fought against the laser rope, the more it sparked and the tighter it held him. At last he stopped moving, and glared at Peri.

'You can't escape, Wild Will,' Peri said, seeing his own face reflected back in the outlaw's deep, black eyes. 'And I won't let you go unless you surrender your guns and promise to leave Buckskinville for good.'

A huge cheer went up all around the town square, echoing off the buildings.

Wild Will spat at him. Peri had to duck to avoid being hit – like all Westrenians, Wild Will was a powerful spitter.

'I won't surrender to a kid like you,' the outlaw said. 'My men will be back from their raid soon – then you'll get what you deserve!'

'I wouldn't count on that,' Peri said. 'But I'm guessing you don't want to surrender at all? Then maybe I can change your mind for you!'

Using all his bionic strength, Peri dragged Wild Will over to the well, pushed him into it and let him dangle on the end of the laser lasso. He felt the full weight of the outlaw pulling on the lasso, but the laser rope held. Only the soles of Wild Will's boots could be seen sticking up above the sides of the well.

'Are you going to surrender now, Wild Will?' Peri said.

'No!' The outlaw's voice came echoing up from inside the well, muffled and hollow. 'I will never surrender! Never!

Never! . . . Waaah!' He yelped as Peri let him drop a little lower.

A burst of laughter exploded around the square. People started to come out of their houses. They were smiling and cheering at the tops of their voices and applauding Peri.

'It's all over!'

'I guess that's the end of Wild Will's reign of terror.'

'We should give him a new nickname!'

'How about Useless Will?'

Peri saw three Westrenians march over to the Hole of Death, carrying a rope. Two others went over to the saloon veranda, picked up the dazed form of Stinky Stan and began to lead him away to the sheriff's office. He hardly struggled against them.

More townsfolk gathered around the well to watch.

Peri gave a tug on the rope. 'Are you ready to surrender yet, Will?'

'Never!' came Will's muffled voice.

'We'll see about that!' Peri spun the laser rope round and round, using all his bionic strength.

'Waaaah!' Will said, as he was flung about in the depths of the well. 'Stop it – I feel sick!'

'Is that a surrender?' Peri demanded.

'Please stop while my insides are still inside me . . . I surrender!'

Peri stopped twirling the rope. 'Can you swim, Will?'

'Yes, I can swim, but why –'

Peri switched off the laser lasso's power. There was a howl and a splash – and a roar of laughter from the gathered crowd – as Will fell into the water at the bottom of the well.

'That's a real unusual lasso you got there!' said a Westrenian with pale green scales that were tinted with blue. 'A lasso that comes out of a pistol – I've never seen such a thing in all my life!'

'It's a … new weapon,' Peri said, thinking quickly. 'You can buy them in Dry Gulch City.'

More cheers and applause rose from the crowd as it parted to let through Diesel and Sheriff Lexor, who had just been pulled out of the Hole of Death. Their clothes and faces were streaked with mud.

'Look at me!' Diesel said. 'I need a long, hot shower, followed by a bath, followed by another shower.'

'I could use a wash myself!' Sheriff Lexor said. 'Then a big, juicy steak and some strong, hot coffee! But first things first. Where's that no-good Wild Will?'

'Useless Will!' somebody shouted from the crowd.

'He's in there!' Peri said, pointing at the well.

Splashing, spluttering noises came from within the well.

'Let's get him out,' the sheriff said.

Some of the bystanders got a rope and pulled Will out of the well. He stood sheepishly, with his head hanging low, his fan of scales drooping, water dripping from him.

Some of the crowd moved threateningly towards him. Several aliens raised their fists. One brandished a stick. Another placed his hand on his gun. Will cringed backward.

'No, stop!' the sheriff told the crowd. 'We must do everything right and proper. This town is a place for decent, law-abiding folk. We must not act like outlaws ourselves.'

The crowd backed away and Will looked distinctly relieved.

'Will and his gang took me by surprise,' the sheriff said. 'But that won't happen again.' He looked at Peri. 'I heard it was you who took Will down. That's mighty impressive for someone so young. It takes a lot of guts to stand up to mean individuals like these.'

'I stood up to them too!' Diesel said. 'I would have done more if Peri hadn't run off and left me.'

'Yes, you told me about that down in the Hole, son,' the sheriff said. 'About thirty-five times! But where's the rest of Will's band of outlaws?'

'They're just coming,' Peri said, pointing.

His superhuman vision had picked them out before anyone else did. The outlaws were shuffling into the square at the far end, all roped together. They were led by Selene, Dexter, Spike and Gunner, with the four guards from the mail coach.

Peri felt a surge of relief. It looked like all the training had worked, and no one had been hurt.

He turned to Will. 'So do you agree to leave town with all your men and to never come back?'

Will nodded, but Sheriff Lexor shook his head. 'Oh no, no! These men will stand trial for their crimes. Westrenia has laws that must be respected and the jailhouse is going to be pretty crowded.'

'Hey, Father!' shouted Dexter, breaking into a run. 'Guess what? We captured the gang!'

'You've done well, son,' the sheriff said. He gave Dexter a big thumbs-down sign, and grinned broadly. 'I'm mighty proud of you.'

'I didn't do it all alone!' Dexter said. 'These guys helped me.' He put his arms around the shoulders of Spike and Gunner, who had just caught up with him. Suddenly, they didn't look so scrawny any more.

'That's good to hear. Maybe you three would like to be my deputies from now on!' the sheriff said.

'That'd be great!' Dexter exclaimed. 'But I must tell you that these three kids from

– from *distant parts,* they did the most. We couldn't have done it without them!'

'I thank you all on behalf of Buckskinville,' the sheriff said to Peri, Diesel and Selene. 'Tonight we're going to have ourselves a big celebration feast, and we'd be mighty happy if you would be our guests of honour!'

Peri took a sly glance at the control strip. His crew had only three days left until they were due back at the IF Space Station.

'Thank you, Sheriff, but we were just passing through and we can't stay,' he said. 'There's somewhere we need to be – and it's rather a long way from here.'

Chapter 10

'I can't wait to get clean!' Diesel said. His band of hair was the colour of mud, and Peri knew that it hadn't changed to that colour by itself. 'I can't stand all this mud on me, it's *shunkelvr'adroj!*'

'What does *shunkel* . . . *shunk* . . . What does *that* word mean?' Selene asked.

'It's Martian for "horrible",' Diesel replied.

'Well, you don't have long to wait,' Peri

said. 'As soon as we're far enough away so they can't see us from town, we'll enlarge the *Phoenix*. Then you can have your shower.'

'And bath!' Diesel added. 'And second shower!'

They marched on over the sandy ground, with the tall cactus plants casting eerie shadows. For some reason, Peri felt uneasy again, but couldn't quite put his finger on why. Perhaps he was just anxious about the time.

'I hope we're going to make it!' Selene said, as if reading Peri's thoughts. 'We don't have much time to make it back to the Milky Way. I'll try to find a few shortcuts.'

'We should be all right,' Peri said. 'But we'll need to go Superluminal. Anyway, it was worth the detour, wasn't it? That was a pretty cool adventure.'

'That's easy for you to say,' Diesel said. 'You didn't spend most of the time in a filthy, hot hole –'

Peri raised his hand. 'Ssshh!'

He realised now why he'd been feeling uneasy – there was a rustling sound coming from the nearby ditch.

'Somebody's following us,' he said under his breath.

'Do you think one of Will's gang escaped?' whispered Selene.

'Let's not take any chances,' Peri muttered.

He pointed to the ditch and counted down on his fingers. 3 . . . 2 . . . 1!

They ran to the ditch, where a figure in a cowboy hat was crouching. Peri, Diesel and Selene jumped down into the ditch and wrestled the alien to the ground.

'You're outnumbered!' Peri said. 'Do you give in?'

The head beneath the cowboy hat nodded. Peri whipped off the hat and saw the startled face of . . .

'Dexter!' Selene said. 'What are you doing here?'

'I didn't mean any harm – I just wanted to see you take off in your space-boat!'

'Ship, not boat,' Peri said.

Diesel looked accusingly at Peri. 'You told him? That's against IF rules!'

'We can trust Dexter,' Peri said.

'That's right, I won't tell a living soul,' Dexter said. 'Can't I just take a tiny peek?'

'He *has* earned it, hasn't he?' Peri said to the others.

'Of course he has,' Selene said.

Diesel nodded grudgingly. 'I suppose.'

'Come on, then,' Peri said.

They all climbed out of the ditch.

'I think we're far enough away now.' Peri placed the *Phoenix* on a patch of clear ground. 'Stand well back, everyone – it's going to get a *lot* bigger!'

He twisted the 'Expansion Packs' dial on his control strip.

And the ship began to grow.

Dexter gasped. 'That is just a plain, plumb impossible miracle!'

Soon the vast oval shape of the *Phoenix* dwarfed them. Its smooth surface shone like silver fire in the afternoon sun.

The door silently opened and there stood Otto. He had his hands on his hips, with all four elbows sticking out angrily. He craned his long crimson neck towards them.

'About time! And who's this you've brought with you?' Otto boomed.

'Oh my goodness!' Dexter said. 'Is that the same alien I saw when he was an insect?'

'What do you mean, insect?' Otto said furiously.

'Sorry,' Dexter said, taking off his hat. 'I only meant I saw you when you were little. I sure am delighted to make your acquaintance, Mr Alien, sir.'

'I'm not an alien,' Otto said. 'You are.'

'We're all aliens here, except for Dexter,' Peri pointed out. 'It's his planet.' He turned to Dexter. 'Would you like to come on board and see what it's like inside?'

Otto spread out his long arms to bar the way. 'He can't come aboard – we don't have time!'

Dexter looked uncertain. 'Is he – I mean, is it going to be safe?'

'Oh, don't mind Otto,' Selene said. 'He looks scary, but he's not really evil.'

'Well, he is a *bit* evil,' Diesel said.

'But you'll be safe with us,' Peri said. 'Come on!'

They went up the ramp and Otto reluctantly moved aside to let them pass.

Peri grinned at how awestruck Dexter was. The alien boy's mouth was open in a permanent 'O' of wonder as he walked along the mauve-lit corridors, touching the smooth, curved walls.

'Come and see the Bridge!' Peri said.

A section of wall slid open and they entered the nerve centre of the ship. Dexter gazed around at the seats that rose up from the deck and the giant, hovering control panel with its display of winking lights and banks of monitor screens.

'Oh, this is like the greatest dream ever!' Dexter said.

An idea came to Peri. 'How would you like to take a trip with us? Just a quick one, to see a little bit of outer space?'

Dexter's face glowed with excitement. 'Oh, I'd love that more than anything else in the whole of Westrenia!'

'Only if you promise to never, *ever* tell anyone,' Diesel said.

'I promise!'

'Sit here, like this.' Peri showed Dexter to a seat. Dexter gave a yelp of surprise as an astro-harness snaked around him.

They all sat down at their stations. Peri beckoned the control panel over, initiated the lift-off sequence and pressed the pyramid-shaped button.

The *Phoenix* took off from the desert and the silent g-force pressed them all back in their seats. In the 360-monitor, Westrenia fell away. Within just a few seconds, it looked like a tiny globe.

'Yeehah!' Dexter shouted, taking off his hat and waving it around.

'We'll just take a quick trip around the moons!' Peri said, smiling at both Dexter's excitement, and his own.

After all the danger they'd experienced on Westrenia, it was great to be reminded that being a Star Fighter was the most fun in the world!

No, Peri corrected himself, *it's the most fun in the entire universe!*

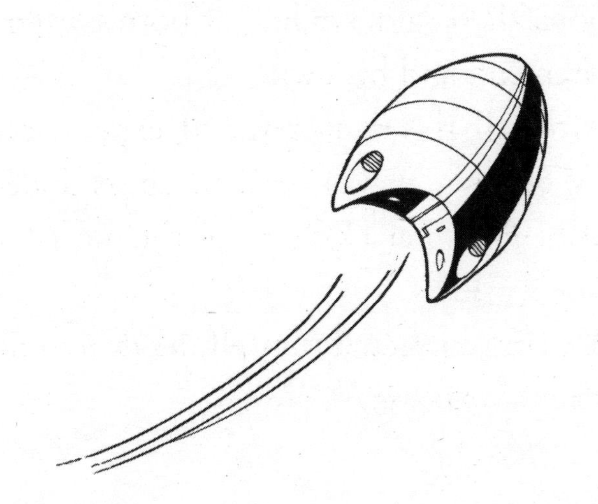

In case you missed the first
STAR FIGHTERS book . . .

Peri and Diesel are drawn into a
dangerous battle with Xion spaceships.

Can they make it back home alive?

Find out! In . . .

Turn over to read Chapter 1

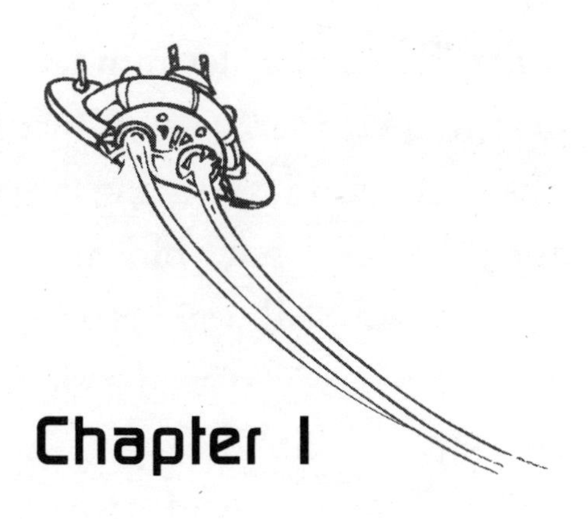

Chapter 1

'Eat dust, alien invader,' Peri shouted as the asteroid shattered into a million glittery pieces.

This sure beats the simulator, he thought as he swerved left then jetted upwards to avoid the asteroid's fiery remains.

Right now he was millions of miles from the Intergalactic Force Space Station, and even further from planet Earth. Up ahead was a bright-blue planet surrounded by shimmering ice rings . . . Saturn! Peri could barely believe his eyes.

Ping! The sonar let him know that their next target was within firing range. It wasn't as good as saving Earth from an alien attack, but blowing up cosmic rubbish was still way better than any 3-D game he'd ever played. He'd blasted an ancient TV satellite, and zapped an old rocket booster. And that asteroid had been totally obliterated.

'Try to keep the pod steady this time, you lamizoid,' Diesel shouted.

Peri glanced over at Diesel, who was swivelling the D-Stroy lasers in the weapon turret. He noticed the gunner wasn't wearing his astro-harness, so any sudden manoeuvre would knock the Martian right off his seat. Peri grinned. He banked as hard as he could. 'Woo-hooo!'

Whack-slam! Diesel flipped out of his seat.

'*Ch'açh!*' he cursed. Diesel always spoke his native language when he was angry – which was most of the time. The gunner's yellow eyes were flashing. The band of hair that stretched across his head was bristling. When he was mad, Diesel sure looked more Martian than human, though in fact he was both.

'You made me miss my target!' he yelled. 'I told them to give me a second-year pilot.

But instead, I get a newbie who knows less than nothing!'

'Chill,' Peri said. 'I'll get us back on track.'

Peri chuckled to himself. A few bruises served him right. That morning Diesel had thrown a galactic fit when he and Peri were paired for a rare Intergalactic Force Academy training mission. The half-Martian was a second-year cadet, a weapons ace and 3-D gaming champion – but he wasn't the brightest star in the constellation.

But Peri agreed with Diesel about one thing – it was odd that a first-year IFA cadet had been chosen. And Peri wasn't even the best in his year – he ranked fourteenth for rocket science and tenth for cosmic combat. So why *had* they selected him?

During the past two weeks he'd pretty much lived in the flight simulator. He practised over and over again until his vision became blurry. But nothing could compare with the real thing – looping the rings of Saturn, or whipping round Pluto.

Suddenly, the pod jerked sharply to the left. Peri's astro-harness snapped him to his seat. Peri struggled to regain control of the steering as the pod looped in a broad U-turn and accelerated.

'What's happening?' Peri's fingers darted over the screens. He engaged the flight stabiliser, checked the energy gauge, and tapped the hologram route finder. 'Nothing's working,' he called to Diesel. 'It's like somebody else is controlling the pod!'

'They must be bringing you back to the Space Station,' Diesel jeered. 'I bet you're in trouble for that stupid stunt you –'

But before he could finish, the pod rocked again, even more violently than before. There was a dull thud beside Peri.

'*Aaargh!*' Diesel roared in pain as he staggered back to his seat clutching his chin. 'I bib ma dung!'

Peri ignored him. He had much bigger things to worry about.

His muscles strained as he wrestled with the anti-drift levers, trying to keep the pod on a steady course while it was batted around like a spaceball. His eyes were drawn to a flashing light on the control board – the red light that signalled a problem with the nuke-fusion-engine. His ears rattled with the piercing robotic voice that warned: 'Danger! Temperature shield overheating. Danger!'

Between jolts, he was able to flip on his

com-unit. 'Mayday! Mayday!' he called. 'IF Space Station – this is TP2-7. Do you copy?'

There was no reply. All Peri heard was the rush of static.

Then, as they rounded Mars, Peri saw something that made his heart nearly rocket out of his chest. Dead ahead, like a galactic roadblock, was a metal sphere the size of Earth's moon. As he watched, thousands of large spikes sprouted from the hull. They were razor-sharp, and at the top of each spike was a viewing platform that looked just like an eyeball. He'd never seen a spaceship like it in any of the textbooks he'd read. Not in *The Big Book of Space*. Or *The Galactic Guide to Gizmos and Gadgets*. Not even in *The Awesome Anthology of Alien Attackers*.

Diesel started yelling in a mixture of Martian and English.

Peri gulped down his fear. 'B-buckle up . . . and shut up!' he snapped.

'You don't give the orders round here! I'm the –' Diesel stopped and gawped at the alien ship. '*S'fâh*,' he muttered. 'That's not from this galaxy.' Diesel scrambled back to his seat and, finally, strapped himself in.

All the navigation systems said the same thing: they were on a collision course with the alien vessel.

'I can't stop the pod!' Peri shouted. 'We're going to crash!'

Which Star Fighter are YOU?

Take the Star Fighter multiple-choice exam to find out . . .

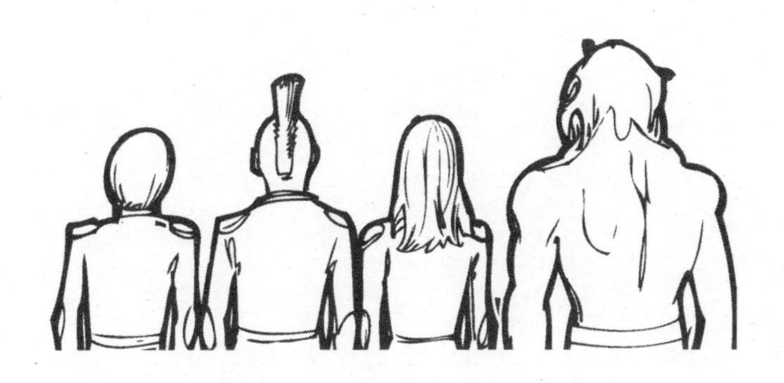

Being a Star Fighter involves making difficult decisions, often at very short notice. Here are ten problems that a Star Fighter might face on a mission. How would YOU react?

Scenario 1

You've been sent to a mirror planet. When you land, your crew see themselves reflected in hundreds of shiny surfaces. Suddenly, the reflection of a shadowy figure appears in the planet's Mirror Maze. What would you do next?

A. Call out to the figure to determine if it's friend or foe. A Star Fighter's first priority is helping others – Peace in Space!

B. Run a scan of the figure and gather facts before proceeding.

C. Follow the reflection and confront the figure immediately.

D. Blast every shiny surface until you find the figure – and then maybe blast the creature too!

Scenario 2

While you're travelling through space, you see a giant floating thumb – a space hitch-hiker needs a lift! But when you look at your scanners, you notice that the alien seems to be hiding itself. What do you do?

A. Invite the hitch-hiker to reveal itself. If it doesn't, surely it can't be trusted.
B. Stop your ship and wait to see if the hitch-hiker reveals itself. Be sure whether it's trying to trick the crew before taking action.
C. Don't stop – it's too risky to engage a hidden alien.
D. Blast the floating thumb – they look stupid!

Scenario 3

You enter the atmosphere of a strange planet and receive a message from an alien commander, demanding that you disable your weapons systems before landing. Do you:

A. Comply with his wishes – diplomacy at all times is the IF way.
B. Obey the command, but keep at least one hand-held weapon in your belt . . . just in case.
C. Put the weapons systems on 'Sleep' mode, so they can be reactivated quickly if needed.
D. Refuse the demand. A warrior never disables his weapons!

Scenario 4

During a mission, two members of your crew start arguing. It looks like it may become a fight before long and disharmony can be a big problem on a ship. How do you solve the situation?

A. Step between the fighting crew members and encourage them to talk through their differences. There will be no disharmony on *your* spaceship.
B. Let them get their issues off their chests, but if they roll anywhere near the controls, you'll step in to take care of matters yourself.
C. Get involved – you like nothing more than winning a good argument.
D. Bash them both over the head – the best way to end a fight.

Scenario 5

Everything's going well on your latest mission, until you notice that you've veered off course. The gravitational pull of outer space is preventing you from flying in a straight line. How do you get back on course?

A. Increase the size of the ship – making it heavier in weight will stop gravity sweeping it away.
B. Go straight to the engine room. Once the problem is found, it can be fixed.
C. Find another route – outer space must be respected.
D. Start blasting. Let's see how gravity likes it when *you* attack!

Scenario 6

While travelling back to planet Earth, you receive a distress call from a ship stranded in the next galaxy. You should have just enough fuel to help them and to get safely back to Earth yourself. What decision do you make?

A. Help them, of course.
B. Try to help them via the com-screen first, to save fuel.
C. Send a message to the command centre, to arrange a rescue party. You can't risk the embarrassment of getting stranded yourself.
D. Leave them stranded – only fools get lost in space.

Scenario 7

You're escorting a diplomat to his home planet, with strict instructions to be back on planet Earth within three days. On the way the diplomat suggests a detour to a different planet, where he can pick up something that's owed to him. What do you do?

A. Politely refuse – a mission is a mission.
B. Remind the diplomat that you are in charge. There won't be any detours.
C. Find out if this planet would be any fun before making a decision. There's no point taking a boring detour, is there?
D. Make sure there's something in it for you before agreeing.

Scenario 8

The autopilot function on your ship breaks down in the middle of the night. Someone needs to be at the controls to keep you on course. How do you handle this problem?

A. Organise the crew into equal shifts, so that responsibility and sleep are evenly shared.
B. Chug a fizzy drink – this is going to be a long night!
C. Keep quiet and hope no one asks you to stay up all night.
D. Pretend to not wake up.

Scenario 9

Disaster strikes when you realise you haven't packed enough food to last your whole mission. What course of action do you take to ensure the crew has sufficient energy?

A. Send an SOS back to the command centre, asking for a space-pod with provisions to be sent to meet you at an agreed location. Safety first!

B. Figure out how long your rations will last. Then check if you'll be passing a space-market any time soon. If you will, there's nothing to worry about.

C. Don't panic – you always have food stashed in your room!

D. Find the nearest spaceship and hijack it, even though they might not have any food that you like!

Scenario 10

You've successfully completed a mission for the IF and are making your way home, when you're surprised by an asteroid belt in outer space. Do you:

A. Take the long way round – your ship is too valuable to risk.
B. Figure out if you can weave your way through the belt – no one ever becomes an IF legend by turning down a challenge!
C. Fly through it – you're very confident in your navigational skills.
D. Blast the asteroids – big lumps of rock never hit back.

Check your answers

Mostly As

You're like Peri – your first instinct is to uphold the code of the Intergalactic Force, ensuring Peace in Space at all times!

Mostly Bs

You're like Selene – you respect the IF code, but like to do things your own way sometimes.

Mostly Cs

You're like Diesel – you never turn down a chance for glory.

Mostly Ds

You're like Otto* – there aren't many problems that can't be solved with a weapon. Most Star Fighters would think twice about travelling with you!

* Technically Otto isn't a Star Fighter, but he is an important part of the *Phoenix* crew!

Have you checked out the **STAR FIGHTERS** website?
It's the place to go for games, downloads,
sneak previews and lots of cosmic fun! You can:

★ Blow up cosmic rubbish and shatter asteroids into a zillion pieces! Practise cosmic combat with the Star Blasters game!

★ Read all about your favourite cadets!

★ Download the Intergalactic Galaxy System Map!

★ Teleport your desktop to the IFA Space Station with out-of-this-world wallpapers!

★ Sign up for the Intergalactic Academy Force newsletter to get space-tastic extras and enter members-only competitions!

And there's much, much more so shuttle off to WWW.STARFIGHTERBOOKS.COM now!